The
Widow's Quilt

The
Widow's Quilt

Poems
Fran Castan

Introduction by William Matthews

Canio's Editions

Acknowledgments

Thanks to the editors of the following magazines and anthologies in which these poems appeared, sometimes in a different form and/or with a different title: *Ailanthus*: "Waving." *The Awards Bulletin of The Poetry Society of America* as recipient of the Lucille Medwick Award: "Operation Crazy Horse." *Blue Unicorn*: "Soundings." *The Doll House* (Pushcart Press, Wainscott, New York: 1995): "Dwelling." *In Celebration of Babies* (Ballantine Books, New York: 1987): "The Adoption." *Ms.* Magazine: "The Adoption," "From an Undeclared War Zone: The Box." *On Prejudice: A Global Perspective* (Anchor/Doubleday, New York: 1993): "To Hannah Vo-Dinh, A Young Poet." *Out of Season* (Amagansett Press, Amagansett, New York: 1993): "Airborne," "Operation Crazy Horse," "Stillbirth." *Pivot*: "Breathing," "How Little Is at Stake," "Operation Crazy Horse," "Washing Up." *The Seasons of Women* (Norton, New York: 1995): "The Adoption." *Violet*: "The Visit," "Unveiling the Vietnam Memorial." *Without Child* (Lexington Books, Massachusetts: 1988): "The Adoption."

Excerpts from the song, *My Blue Heaven*, © 1927 Copyright Renewed 1955. Written by Walter Donaldson and George Whiting. Donaldson Publishing Company and George Whiting Publishing. International Copyright Secured. All rights reserved. Used By Permission.

Heartfelt thanks to the poets—friends and teachers—who have enriched my life and encouraged the work in this book: Philip Appleman, Jillian Blume, Robert Bly, Siv Cedering, Diana Chang, Jan Freeman, Rita Gabis, Daniela Gioseffi, Robert Hass, Florence Howe, Galway Kinnell, Naomi Lazard, William Matthews, Sharon Olds, Myra Shapiro, and the East End Poetry Workshop.

Many thanks to The MacDowell Colony and the Virginia Center for the Creative Arts, for the marriage of solitude and fellowship.

Profound gratitude to Sag Harbor's treasure, Canio Pavone, for his open door and for his support of artists of all persuasions.

Unwavering love and thanks to my grandparents and parents; to my aunt and uncles; to Dan, Jane and Steve; to Cindy and Tammy; to Callie and Sierra; for the lessons they have taught and the joy they have given.

Cover painting, "The Widow's Quilt," by Lewis Zacks.

ISBN 1-886435-04-9

Copyright © 1996 by Fran Castan

Library of Congress Catalog Card Number: 96-83170

Canio's Editions
P.O. Box 1962
Sag Harbor, N.Y. 11963
(516) 725-4926

In memory of Sam Castan
May 12, 1935 - May 21, 1966

For Lewis Zacks
whose love made me lucky twice

Contents

III. Starting Over

Introduction

The Gift Returned

"The widow always wears a black coat," Fran Castan begins her poem, "Soldier's Widow: A Generic Photo." There's not an "I" in the poem.

The widow has a role to play. "She is here to receive the flag." Her deadpan tone and primer sentence structure (*See Spot run. See Spot grieve.*) allow her to play that role without smothering in it, thanks to an offhand irony: "Valium/ is the drug of choice for such occasions."

What if she should, however muffled, be tempted to cry out, or to collapse? "Two men, solid as a pair of bookends,/ flank her and grip her arms."

The eulogy will be given to whom it may concern and the folded flag, the widow's quilt, to her.

One reason there's not an "I" in the poem is that Castan knows the experience is not hers alone. Well, the state had its brash rights in the matter, and her husband had parents and siblings, each with privacies and deprivations. But I'm thinking, as these poems do, of something even larger and more terrifyingly obvious than that. The war was given to all of us, and took something from all of us, and most of us felt the exchange was uneven, no matter what our individual politics were then. Castan's title poem invites us all to be widows and to sleep under our flag and to wake from our fitful dreams alone with America.

Castan has contrived, in and by means of these poems, a separate peace. I have concentrated in my brief introduction on her poem that contains the title phrase because it proposes both the widow's and the country's psychic labor, balancing the private and political with exemplary dexterity. But the book is full of private braveries made public by Castan's skilled tussles with our common wealth—our language.

And here's a happy irony: isn't it the case now (look at her dedication), when she can return the quilt in the form of this fine book, that
> two men, solid as a pair of bookends,
> flank her and grip her arms?

—*William Matthews*

From an Undeclared War Zone: The Box

Under crumpled letters and old books,
under hard bits of rubber bands,
under paper clips huddled
in contorted shapes,
like a pile of corpses
whose bones angle and break,
the dress startles me.
It is my daughter's first,
pale yellow
with cherries stitched by hand
above the scalloped hem.
One underarm is ripped
along a seam I meant to fix
last time I opened the box.
And I did plan to wash it and press it
and save it in heavy duty plastic
the way one cares for an heirloom.
But I always leave my daughter's dress
exactly where I find it,
under her father's unframed photo,
under his wristwatch,
under his notes
made in a Vietnamese field,
their blue ink spattered with sepia—
his dried blood. Close the lid!

My hands do not obey.
They seize the empty dress.
They know its true heritage:

3

the sheer, sweet shape of our daughter
crumpled and torn,
heaped with remnants
of the life and death of her young father,
in a box no different from my mind,
trained to accept this mad legacy
from the time I was five,
in our kitchen in Brooklyn,
listening to my grandma cry,
"Cossacks! Cossacks!"
They are still riding
toward the house of her childhood
as she holds my hand....I shove
my daughter's first dress
into the coffee grinds,
chuck out the kitchen garbage,
as if I could scatter a century
memorized with our hands.

I. Childhood

"You'll see a smiling face,
a fireplace, a cozy room,
A little nest that's nestled
where the roses bloom."

Dwelling

The first house you left dreams.
In the belly of the sink, in the eye of the glass,
in the arms of the old wing chair, it asks
"What has become of you?" It abides

like the snail's spent shell
swirled in the shape of seasons gone
and come again, as the planet whirls on
to sleep in its own shadow, only

to shine again in the sun. You
must return to that dwelling in the dark,
take memory back,
and, this time, learn to live by heart.

Old Photo

My father stands on the rocky lakeside
in rubber bathing sandals and brief,
belted swimtrunks. His left hand
holds a cigarette, his right arm carries me,
in a robe of white terry with a single
star on the breast pocket.
I am not clinging, just
resting on his summer skin.
On the photo back, still distinct,
in blue-black Waterman's ink,
his neat, unadorned script rolls
evenly forward, regularly spaced and straight.
I imagine him in a room I can't remember,
turning over this photograph
and imagining me, in a room he's never seen,
coming across his words, as I do today,
"Franny, two, and Daddy at Green Mansions."
His ambition for recording our journey
gave out, gave in to the white paper sack
crammed with photos.
I uncurl one at a time, tape it
to the west wall of the house
in the afternoon sun
to make a fresh image of us.
As the camera zooms in,
father and I look back so trustingly;
I want to swoop us up and carry us
into a safe and orderly life.

Wing Chair

From my hiding place
under the wing chair,
I see my mother's helpless
house slippers, her legs
pale and speckled
as the morning oatmeal.
I see my father's heavy
workshoes, his itchy trousers.

My father says he only
borrowed the money
for his playground, a baize table,
where he lifted me, his alibi,
to watch brightly colored balls
collide in smoky cones of light,
while men he nickled and dimed with
dribbled cigarette kisses,
bet I'd break hearts.

My father says he only
borrowed the money
from the cash drawer
just for an hour during lunch
so he could take it to a horse,
a sure way to double it,
and he could put it all back,
no one hurt, the rent paid.

My father says he only

9

borrowed the money
for bills and bills
devouring more bills
than those he earns each week
and counts out as if his counting
would change the sum.

My father says, if only
his boss had come later,
after lunch, to check the till.
My father says, wouldn't you
know his luck,
even with a winner, he lost.

In the arms of the wing chair,
I whisper the story
to an embroidered woman
who strolls on the golden bridge,
her parasol open,
her hair in a geisha's knot.
Because I do not mention *luck*,
the woman does not cry,
and if she did, who would mind
in the soundproof world
of cloth?

Mother's Song

Don't answer the bell.
They'll think we're not home.
Otherwise they'll take everything—
the couch, the table, even the beds,
and we'll be out in the street,
in the rain,
no roof, no toilet. Just the sewer.
So be like a mouse—
small and quiet, secret and dark.
If the phone rings and it's Mr. Fox,
say we sent the check yesterday.
And if he wants to talk to me,
I'm not home and Daddy's not home.
You're here all by yourself.

These are the Current Events.
Forget Korea,
the 38th Parallel,
Pusan, Pork Chop Hill,
The North, The South,
The Reds, The Pinkos.
Forget the map, its latitudes,
the juicy dictionary fat with meanings,
ambiguities,
paradox,
fate.

Stay home where the heart is

walled in by four rooms,
pale green paint curling
like leaves growing long,
exposing the flower
of red paint beneath.
Stay here, near me.
But if I wave my hand,
go to the door
and in your baby mouse voice
say you are all alone.

Children's Matinée: 1945

After cartoons and a double feature,
we watch the newsreel.
My babysitter whispers, "This is real.
Those people are dead.
The Germans killed them
because they are Jews, like us."

I'm six. I have no mask
of understanding, no disguise
of acceptance. I watch a bulldozer
shove naked people into a ditch
and cover them with white powder.
I know they are still alive.
Every single part of them hurts.
They are so embarrassed
without their clothes.
Men and women together,
not even in the same family.
They are so thin we can see shapes
we didn't know people had,
like the two bones at the chicken's knee
Grandma breaks to make soup,
bones that fit neatly into each other,
like my new molars, when I chew.

And the babies! My mother would never

believe this. She won't even let me
hold my new brother. His head is so soft
it could split, like an egg.

At home, I cry to Grandma.

"Zohrgzikh nisht. Zohrgzikh nisht.
"Don't worry. Don't worry.
The people in the newsreel
do not feel the bulldozer.
They are dead
and we are in America.
That's why we came here, to be safe."

"What if the Germans come here, too,
   Grandma?"

"Look at you. You're beautiful.
Blond hair. Blue eyes.
A little *shiksa*.
You were born here.
You speak English.
Nobody believes you're Jewish."

I watch her brush the dark
river of hair she coils
tightly in place at her neck,
watch her pinch olive cheeks
so they bloom briefly pink,
watch her flatten curly brows

above eyes mysteriously flecked
like dark micas with chips of gold,
listen to her brag to her sister:
"Mein goldena, my little gold one,
even in Russia, in the pogrom of 1905,
they would leave this one alone."

How can she separate me
from my whole family, link me
with the enemy, place me
among her own murderers,
just so one of us can live?

Automat

We dolls were AWOL, Mom and me,
Absent Without Leave from Grandma,
out of the prison of her kitchen,
where grief was served up with the meat,
where each bite eaten,
no matter how well seasoned,
made us sick with sorrow
for the life she let us know she lost
to make ours possible.

We spun glass doors
with a wand marked *Push*
and entered a space
lofty as a theatre, and balconied.

We raised brass-rimmed windows,
small as picture post cards,
to remove still lifes within:
scoop of egg salad, slice
of chocolate layer, cube of strawberry jello.
We choo-chooed brown trays on silver rails
to *Beverages*, clicked our mocha-colored cups,
dropped Indian-head nickels in the slot,
pressed porcelain buttons,
and out the spout,
shaped like a generous mouth,
coffee streamed with or without cream.
Mom smiled like a friend
you could leave the house with and be free.

Washing Up

My father hung his windbreaker
on the doorknob of the closet
it was too dirty to go into
and walked directly to the bathroom.
I followed, like any duckling
safe within the widening V of its drake,
then sidled between him and the sink.

He surveyed the day's leavings: black
arcs under his nails, jaunty as French berets
on fingers he wiggled like ten dancers.
Between the taps, hot, cold, and back,
he rocked his hands. Rhythm
kept them from burning or freezing
under the separate spigots.

The berry-colored bar of Lifebuoy,
or the drab green of Palmolive,
rolled in his hands until it whitened
and dropped back into the dish.
On the stains that remained,
he sprinkled Dif, white and powdery
as the Bon Ami mother used to scour the sink,
and, with a brush, scrubbed it deep

into his calluses, as if their bubbled surface
were the bottom of a burnt pot.

When he was done, he reached for pumice.
Sometimes he'd attack with tweezers, or
a sewing needle heated red-blue on the gas jet,
dark splinters lodged in his skin—steel
he welded onto wartime vessels
at the Brooklyn Navy Yard.

I grabbed each coarse cleanser
to be just like him. But he wanted my hands
pink as the hands of a lady-in-training,
my rayon dress embroidered with flowers,
my long blond braids woven with grosgrain,
my Mary Janes thickly-coated with chalky
Sani-White polish, my Ivory Snow hands
pampered by his labor down at the docks
with rough men who cursed and played cards.

Authority

My grandmother was beaten
by her own father for reading
in the wrong language. In Zhitomir,
in the *shtetl*, you could read
Hebrew or Yiddish, not Russian.
If you were a girl,
you need only read enough
to light the Shabbos candles
or say the holiday prayers.
Grandmother yearned for beauty,
squeezed elderberries into whitewash,
painted her room until it glowed
pink as clouds above the setting sun.
Who did she think she was,
trading her father's rice
for a Russian book?

My mother was always reading.
Daughter of her mother,
what choice did she have?
Each week she walked
to the New Utrecht Branch
of the Brooklyn Public Library.
Mother yearned for knowledge.
She read the latest theories
of child care. The authors were men,
a new breed. Experts
who invented "The Feeding Schedule,"

a four-hour interval
they pronounced "Ideal."

As my cries grew to howls,
as her tender breasts
engorged, Mother watched the clock,
dutifully waiting, earnestly wanting us
to be models of the new order.
When the merciful fourth hour concluded
and I had cried myself
through stages of distress
to a fitful sleep, she would wake me.
It would take a long time
to trust the body I found myself in
to bring forth my own voice
as if, for the first time, it could be heard.
Granddaughter and daughter
of these women, I am usually writing.
What choice do I have?

Emergency Bracelet

When her friend died alone,
my mother provided a set of keys
"Just in case." I carried them
in my pocket, where they chimed.
I pulled them out by the blue heart,
leather embossed with a red flower
she must have chosen for the occasion.
She must have wanted me
to hold this amulet as
I opened the door to find her.

I broke the golden rule,
unzipped her purse, searched
for the social security card
I needed to place her in a home.
I found another card in clear plastic
scrawled in her own hand,
"If needed, call my daughter,"
and like the vein
scribbling across her wrist,
my name, frail and blue.

Elegy: What I Failed to Tell the Gambler

Yellow wings of Cordero,
chameleon on Shoemaker's back,
Larkspur, you'd whisper.
Eight. Three. Eight.
Luck was your lady.
How you'd court her.
How she'd cheat.

While you chased her,
I coaxed you. Perched
on your freckled back, small
fists pounding gid-dap,
my head—ringleted—
in the curve of your neck,
I could feel the wild thing caged.

Each day at the starting gate,
each horse in blinders,
one kiss from your sweetheart
and Turcotte trots
into the winner's circle,
his silks pinned by a fine-boned
lady, or, when Luck's fickle,
he falls to the sudden track,
where there are no lengthy
infidelities.

All you asked could be answered

in a single race, and asked again.
In the slow pace of days
you had no patience
for what you could not see. But night
has always kept a ledger
posted by the moon—gold and silver
accruals that seem to vanish
but just change hands—like love
you gave me, how much
I gave you back—more
than we could ever squander.

This Body

I hold my mother in the bath
the way she used to hold
a plucked pullet in a tub of hot water
to ease out the last feathers,
stubborn ones at the tip of the wing,
at the base of the thigh,
where slippery skin covers and uncovers
a white hinge of bone. My mother's spine,
her rib cage, her winged shoulders
protrude like an embryo's
into skin the color of pale yolk.

Remember the evening gowns of the '40's,
Rita Hayworth's lamés
rippling over her sexy body?
Those were the costumer's glory days,
gold draped in loose folds
upon each hip. From a criss-cross
at the waist, gold puckering up
to each breast. O,
the nightmare of my mother
in a slinky gown made of her own skin.
"This body," she says, "This body,"
the way you'd admonish
a naughty child or a disobedient dog,

expecting no immediate answer.
"This body," already draped
in a shroud of its former glamour,
calls me forth
as it did the first time,
when the allure of its curves, its pheromones,
set to music my father's cries
and bid me enter
her body, my life.

II. Woman, Wife, Widow

"Just Mollie and me
And baby makes three.
We're happy in my
blue heaven."

Souvenir

As he rolls over and back
and over again, restless as a dune
that climbs itself to some new level of comfort,
sand from Hawaii shifts
in the glass cube on the nightstand
and again streaks his forearms
with skeletal specks of others—
shark skull, walrus tusk, scallop shell,
bits of whatever stays hard, armbone
of a mollusk-lover of another age—grit
he holds me against in his arms,
made of the arms of others who have lain down;
their clingings join with our own and are saved,
as if sand could keep us from vanishing.

Airborne

Inside the sealed cabin, where gravity
leans hard against my chest
and there is only the usual recycled air,
I feel desperately short of breath.
Overhead, the plastic nozzle is
useless, an umbilical stump.

I remember her, decades ago,
in the seventh month of our life together,
when she stopped moving inside me.
The doctor listened for her heartbeat.
As he turned away, I knew she was dead.
He sent me home to wait.
It took a whole week for labor to start.

And do you know, I continued to smile
at the "Good Mornings," the pleasure
total strangers display when they notice
a pregnant woman. I ate and slept
as if she were still sheltered,
as if she could be delivered.

On that eerie birthday when she came forth
to the sound of my cry only,
those who thought they were being kind

pushed me back against the table,
forced a mask on me, took from me
my awareness. All I know of her
in the air is her body,
silken, absolutely still,
growing cool against my thigh.
I wanted to see her, just once,
and to give her a coverlet
of earth.

Stillbirth: A Revised Elegy

Child, who condensed the human drama
to a single act, who cheated Death
out of the usual anticipation,
the myriad scenarios of
how and *when.*
Efficient one—
economic of time and space—
shaping me to both cradle and coffin.
And why not? What better way to die
than in a mother's arms,
if not in utero?
Is my tone odd? Probably.
It's that of a woman, a wife,
who gave birth to Death.
Woman, wife—both require a child.
Ask the Hebrew chroniclers
who gave birth to Birth,
who commanded, "Be fruitful and multiply."
Those ancestors are not unique.
Arab queens have been cast off for being barren
or for giving birth to daughters, only.
My clever one—my silent daughter—
she thumbed her nose at the whole show.

Breathing

In a sunlit corner, I sit with the dog
and listen to our breathing.
I like to think my breath
goes all the way to her heart, to her tail,
to the park, where she runs it around a tree.
Every breath is borrowed:
all the breaths ever taken, ever to be
taken, are somewhere in this world.
When life seems an inherent unsuccess, failing,
as it does, in the end, at least as we know it,
I push out my belly in this great exchange,
breathe deep
with those who've gone and those to come.

The Adoption

I remember the quiet room, the dark
green chair where we sat afternoons,
the sun—no matter how tightly shuttered out—
coming in and curving across us
as if we were not separate, but a single body
joined in a ceremony of light.
My legs beneath you,
my arms around you, my breast
under the glass bottle with rubber nipple,
I talked to you and sang to you.
No one interrupted us.
The dog sat quietly in the corner.
If I could have given birth to you,
I would have. I would have taken you
inside me, held you
and given birth to you again.
All the hours we spent in that room. Then,
one day, with your eyes focused on mine, you
reached up and stroked my cheek. Your touch
was that of the inchworm on its aerial thread
just resting on my skin, a larval curve
alighting and lifting off, a lightness
practicing for the time it will have wings.
I like to think wherever you go, you will
keep some memory of sunlight in the room
where I first loved you, and you first loved.

Operation Crazy Horse

A grand Kowloon hotel. A hedge
of red hibiscus. A tiled pool.
A masseuse who pressed fragrant
oil of almond into my body
in the full heat of the sun.
Elsewhere, northwest of Saigon,
a man beheld you, and fired.

At the undertaker's you were
all made up and your hair
was parted wrong, so I smoothed it
the way you would have liked.
Someone shouted *Stop*, as if we were
caught making love on the couch
in my father's house. God knows

what they feared. Unfamiliar
streaks in your hair must have paled
at the moment of terror
and grown longer in the time since,
eerie as strands of ticker tape
still printing. Such dark hair
shocked white. How afraid you were.
All I could do was hold you.

Soldier's Widow: A Generic Photo

The widow always wears a black coat.
She is cold in this coat even in summer.
She is here to receive the flag.
She is here to say hers is a small sacrifice
for God and for country. Valium
is the drug of choice for such occasions.
She will not cry out. She will not collapse.
Two men, solid as a pair of bookends,
flank her and grip her arms.
They wear dark suits or other uniforms.
"Hero," is the theme of the eulogy,
as if her husband chose to give his life.
Tonight, she will sleep with the widow's quilt,
the folded flag taken from his coffin.

Unveiling the Vietnam Memorial

In the failing light, survivors
found the name they sought
cut in the polished stone
and they stroked it
as if it were a person.
I watched on television,
far from that monument, far
from your grave.
If I do nothing
to release myself from this pain,
I will never forget you.
In the village of my body,
I, too, am a burn victim,
draped in wet skin.
And I will be buried as you were,
unhealed, as were the others—
Americans and Vietnamese.

Remember our dog?
She rolled in feathers, in leaves,
even dried turds—anything
to disguise herself, to stalk her prey.
How did we learn
to make a monument to some
and to call others enemy,

to conceal our species from itself?
With the body of each warrior
we place in the earth,
we etch ourselves most truly
into the cold memory of stone: the acid
history of our kind, which murders its own.

III. Starting Over

"A turn to the right,
  a little white light
Will lead you to my
  blue heaven."

The Visit

I.

On the ground beside you,
I'm on my side of our bed,
plumping up the old quilt
of sedum plants covering you; weeds
I grasp seem to be yanked back,
as though I take too much of the bedding.
I stayed away so long
because my father said visiting a corpse
is barbaric, and my heart
can find its way to yours
from any place. Like a chimpanzee
lifting lice from the close
coat of her mate, I take a white stone
from the grass.

II.

All around us are double graves:
Beloved Husband, Adored Wife.
Some carved dates show
mere days passing between deaths. Souls
who would have walked willingly
into pyramids and lain down.
On that tomb, beside the dead man's name,
is the name of his spouse
still living. And I myself am leaning
on my half of our headboard, on stone
smooth except for my name and birthdate
and the hyphen that waits.

III.

As wind sweeps
untidy pebbles from the path,
I drift below ground. And there you are
in your blue suit, striped shirt, black oxfords
I carried to the undertakers. Tasks
keep the living sane—*living sane*—
a twin impossibility,
like the inability to imagine you
alive or dead.

IV.

See the shape
my body pressed into the long grass
in my place beside your grave
as if it had molted
a shell of itself. This absent part of me
stays with you. My arms
fold themselves around me.
My hands feel my own bones.
These bones coax me
away from yours. They insist
I return to the living.

At the Shore

Go barefoot.
Stay with the sea gull just rising.
Note the black hem on his tail,
the idiosyncratic hook of his beak.
Keep your eye on the breaking line of waves,
steady and abundant.
Never mind what lurks in full sunlight.
Laugh, right now, and for the first time,
at madness. Count yourself among the survivors.
Wink at them.
See the toddler hurl himself toward you and the sea.
Watch his pure delight in the abracadabra of foam.
His left hand locked on his mother's thumb,
he snaps his right on your thumb, as if
he's always known you.
He shrieks with joy
and yanks you forward.

Double Exposure

Hawaii: One

At the baggage desk,
waiting to change planes,
I am given a ticket
for my husband's body
in a Vietnamese crate.
I never see the island,
only stare at Honolulu
stamped on my passport.

Hawaii: Two

At the baggage desk,
suntanned and smiling,
my new husband
buys a string of orchids,
loops them around my neck.
Snorkeling in Hanauma Bay,
we watch parrot fish eat biscuits
from boxes we wave underwater.

Soundings

We are pleura, pure gossamer, a belief
adrift in a boat, pedals
turned by water, rudder
veering of its own accord,
wind against the canopy, and we
let it be, let ourselves be
blown far from the voices, far
from the lakeside radio.
But there is no silence.
The lake ripples. The woods
echo an ice-age basso,
his long vowels pitched moonward
for listeners in the garbled dark.

Nestlings at the Summer House

In a flashlight beam, inches from the rear tire,
we see one on the gravel—flat, except for
the glob of its entrails. We scoop
three live ones into the fallen nest.
Their sheer-skinned bodies throb
like excised hearts.

We put the nest back as high as our arms
can reach from our perch on the fencepost,
in the spirit that pervades us lately,
a giving up of what we cannot solve or save.
We are past the grandiose blaze of youth
when we thought everything was up to us.

This pine was knee-high
in our wedding photo, my daughter, age six,
my husband's sons, ten and twelve,
and we two, blessed by rice. Fearless or foolish,
we gathered them in, made a place
for each, bonded over this brood,

blind to the dangers. Remember
the ornithologist who raised a whooping crane
as if he were its mother—
his flapping arms, strutting legs, wild call
as he tried to teach it the mating posture?
Sometimes it feels like a life no less alien

we have wedded ourselves to.
We latch our seatbelts, my husband's turn
to drive back to the city, mine to dream.
We are the Flying Wallendas,
an old circus family of so many
who have fallen. From cantilevered girders

of a skyscraper-in-progress, we swing
toward our grown children, and away.
They, too, are suspended and swinging
in our routine act with no net.
Just when we wonder how we can get down,
the trapeze lengthens its ropes

and our feet come to rest
perfectly on the ground.
When we look up,
our children are all aloft,
fully glad to be there,
exuberant and unafraid.

A Walk on Madison Avenue

In the passing windows, I see a woman
who stoops, as if she carried yoked buckets.
She keeps my pace and watches me
with the frank gaze of a peasant.
But wait, she is me, firstborn in America,
still close to the old country,
in the ghetto of thought. At our door, Cossacks
breathe and when they enter,
they do not knock.
Though I have never seen them,
their rhythms thrum in my bones
as I pass a window of navy velvet
slashed to display
armless hands and headless necks
for the sparkle of green and white gems.

My sandaled feet snap in step with a past
of whispers, of women poulticing fevers
they would risk dying to cure.
In an endless line beyond me,
in the glass, they watch
that we do not breathe the night
vapors or come too close to the flame.
They have hovered and cooked and washed
in dusty cabins for us,
though they did not know us and would not,
but they had a dream of continuance,
of safety. I hear their prayers

over braided loaves and Sabbath candles,
their chants as wine
spills from humble vessels
onto stone.

Here, on the avenue,
a storefront surrounds our image,
a marble picture frame
whose surface gleams with fossil figures
in a new place. The energy of each
life propels us forward: centuries
of women with wet breasts, the globed
seed of the pomegranate poised
like a ruby between their teeth.
As we lean over the beds of those we love,
all those women are listening with us.

Crone

I could use a merkin*
now that estrogen has taken
its thicket of bristles
to wherever it has gone,
just as it brought them glistening,
tough as whiskers when it came.
Perhaps it would be better
to place a pious cap
on that little pocket of pleasure,
a mini-version of the *sheitl*
my old testament ancestors wore
to cover their heads,
the long glory of their hair
tucked up out of sight, beauty
that might tempt a man,
other than their husbands.
But this pubic wig, this merkin,
might lure another while reminding me
of the times I lost myself
willingly for love
in those full-foliage days
when a beloved's hand
drawn to that tawny pelt
could make me do anything.
O, nothing particularly kinky,

* "Counterfeit hair
for women's privy parts,"
1796, O.E.D.

52

no more or less than most
would do with their bodies
in sheer air for love.
If I agreed with my doctor
that menopause is a deficiency disease,
I'd "do" ERT—
Estrogen Replacement Therapy—
legal drug you can take
until ninety to stay dewy,
and as my bones were lowered
in their thin tent of skin,
a mourner would slip
some tampax in the coffin,
just in case, like food or wine
placed in the death vaults
of believers in eternal life.

Double Manicure at the Breakfast Table

Why these red nails our daughter
    and daughter-in-law insist on?
They file and polish, polish and file,
    compare color, shape, length,
And patterns—unplanned for—that sheets
    and blankets press into damp nails.
They awake and say, "Look at my
    'sheets,' see my 'blankets.'"

With nails still perfect from
    the last manicure,
They skim the week's polish
    onto cotton,
Sail these streaked clouds
    into a basket.
"Shall I wear Red Lady, or do you
    like Deep Ember better?"

They are artists at the table, solving
    problems of the craft:
This chip, that crack, a too-heavy
    enamel streak.
In their vocal duet is concern beyond
    mere vanity,
Urgency of a life's work greater
    than this simple task.

In each small focus of perfection, in each

blood-red globule
They paint with such care, I begin to see
   the shape of their conjuring:
Our grandchild will be
   carried soon
By one of these children,
   these beautiful daughters.

To Hannah Vo-Dinh, a Young Poet

Ever since I returned from the Far East
with our year-old child on my left hip
and a baggage ticket like a hot coal,
a hot coal in my right hand,
I am always half in one world,
half in another, ever since
I dropped that burning coal
at the baggage desk and claimed his body.

Almost round face, yellow-brown eyes,
close-cropped hair,
intelligent, mysterious images, words
chosen with care, Hannah,
Hannah Vo-Dinh, you could be his daughter.

Now that I am older, not a widow of 27,
I am less jealous. I do wish my husband
had made love to another woman, someone,
perhaps, like your own mother.

"If I get my hands on the Gook
who killed your husband, I'll break his neck,
I will, with my own two hands."
I felt so unprotected when my neighbor spoke,
so alone with his hate, his failure
to recognize us as a single species. O, Hannah,

Hannah Vo-Dinh, how I wish,
how I wish you were just a few years older,
then you would be a tangible presence,
a living possibility of my best fantasy:

As you, Daughter,
in your shoes, he still walks.
I will not rest
in this or any other life
until the Vietnamese names
rise on the giant V in Washington,
until they are formed
in the same stone of honor as the American names,
as you are formed, dear
Lotus, of a single, human moment of transcendence.

First Month's Blessing

Granddaughter, if you could look far
you would see our faces
all around the room
admiring you. Our eyes
move to each sweet part—
your hair, your toes, one hand
reaching out like a starfish,
the other, hidden in its tight bud.
Granddaughter, if you could look far
you would understand our work.
Where each eye rests on your body
a little circle of unseen fabric
is laid down and attached
to every other circle,
like the quilts grandmothers made
in some of the "old countries"
and carried here to America.
It is this invisible cloak
you will wear all of your days.
Though no one can say how,
it will keep growing to your exact size,
and whatever happens, it will warm you
and shield you from harm.

Hazelnuts

At 5:00 a.m., I wake as if someone shook me,
someone with many chores and not enough time,
someone I follow to the kitchen,
where I pour water into the pot,
spoon coffee into the brewing basket,
crack the shells of three hazelnuts,
crush and sprinkle them over the ground beans.

And as if she were calling them herself,
my grandmother's children rise.
Could she have imagined them at 88, 84 and 79,
this last day they will all be together?
One is moving away and the two remaining
are too weak to follow. They enter the room
as if they could stop their life-long squabbling,
as if the warring, split-off parts
of my grandmother's self—of any self,
of the collective body of the world's self—
could kiss and make up the way Yassir Arafat
shook hands with Yitzhak Rabin,
calling him cousin, saying after all,
we are all children of Abraham,
we can dwell together in peace.

Perhaps the fragrance of this coffee
can take my grandmother's children
back to Russia in the last hours
of the last century,
back to their places, close to each other

in the floating world of possibilities
she carried inside her,
where one half of each self they would become
waited, as she, a young girl
with a small metal pail hanging from her wrist,
roamed peacefully in the Zhitomir woods,
picking hazelnuts, gathering each cluster,
each trio in their downy covers,
as carefully as if they were three children
asleep on their bellies,
little rumps in the air
under a light green blanket.

I brew this coffee with the faith of a witch,
a woman with power to resurrect
a hazelnut tree, its canopy, its roots
branching out like twin placentas,
one above earth, one below,
to bear my grandmother's children
back to the sheltering flesh of her body
so she can keep them close together
once again, for this last day,
before they separate, as they did the first time,
to go, singly, from one world into the next.

Wedding Anniversary

We wake from our longing
to my breasts, to your sex
swelling between our thighs.

We embrace with death
shimmering in our hair,
skimming its dry net over our bodies,

luring us with its dream
of mothers and fathers—
nebulae of arms and legs,

hands and lips,
all that can hold onto another
reaching from the center

until it seems possible to begin again
inside my own father,
slip from him, pluck myself

from his ecstasy, be
the pull of my mother,
catch in her warmth

as a stunned incipience
among the unparted,
the intact, the not-me,

to witness the burning
of self on self
intent upon a new self—

myself, yourself, we become ourselves
mother, father, the absent
part of each other moving

over the landscape of the body
like the moon not quite catching up
to the watcher's face, yet promising

union we will keep
in or out of these bodies,
just like the stars that die

and merge with one another,
only the sheen of their former selves
filtering down as if they were not

in their conjugal beds,
in their winding sheets of pure light,
giving birth to each other again.

How Little Is at Stake

We are as air.
Here, then gone.
Sand. Stone. Grass.
The green apple floating.
Fisherman's net draped in an eerie "T".
A bird on each post, waiting.

The dog moves from sun to shade and back
in a rhythm. She knows her job.
In a Sunfish, two lovers are rocking.
They have cast themselves into the hands of the air
and they wait. A speedboat
delivers a wake for them to navigate, and they do.

We all wait in the sun and the shade,
in the office and the living room.
We kill time. We pace.
The couple can come ashore, rest
in the dune, make love, hover
a moment out of themselves.

You are near me, breathing quietly
as we wait for whatever will take us,
sleep or apocalypse. We do not say
how much we love, how much it matters
to see the cormorant rise, or the mockingbird
paint her ancient totem on the sky.

Waving

Sun in the water glinted about our shadows
like halos in a dulled painting of saints.
Toward the departing shore, a small figure,
a man in a Boston Whaler, was waving.
No one waved back.
But the man kept waving and waving
and so my hand lifted
and waved back in longer and longer arcs
as we drifted apart and the tears, how they came,
how they came. And I didn't even know him.
And I wondered about this. Why did he need to wave
to the large ferry boat full of people
from his tiny Boston Whaler?
Why did I need to wave back?
Soon, others were waving, too. People
in small pleasure boats were waving and waving.
It was important to be waving.
Safe journey, it said, safe journey.
You will be waved out and waved back.

Colophon

Cover: Oil painting and design by Lewis Zacks
                Layout and Typography by CMYK Design

Typography: Jillian Blume Griggs, JB Graphics

Type: Palatino

Paper: 60 lb. Glatfelter Supple Opaque (Recycled)

Printing: Thomson-Shore, Inc.

Photograph: Author by Ann Chwatsky

Literary Paperback Originals

ANTHONY BRANDT
The People Along the Sand. Three stories, six poems, a memoir. Tales of missed connections and misunderstandings, a memoir of the death of a marriage told with uncompromising honesty and uncommon grace. Introduction by Bill Henderson. $9.95. ISBN 0-9630164-1-5

EDWARD BUTSCHER
Child in the House. A new collection of ferocious, yet human lyrics. Introduction by David Ignatow. $10.00. ISBN 0-9630164-9-0

VIRGINIA CHRISTIAN, HOPE HARRIS, ERIKA DUNCAN
Three Cautionary Tales. Two novellas and one long short story explore that area where beauty and pain meet. $14.00. ISBN 0-9630164-3-1

MARK CIABATTARI
The Literal Truth. Rizzoli Dreams of Eating the Apple of Earthly Delights. Surreal tales of Manhattan and the Hamptons. This 'clever and cartoonish novel is a delightful romp, more Calvino than Kafka.' — Kirkus Reviews. $12.00. ISBN 0-9630164-7-4

PAT FALK
In the Shape of a Woman. Poems by award-winner, Pat Falk. Introduction by Sidney Feshbach. "...this is the form/ we know where we are/ we have come to speak through stone." $12.00. ISBN 1-886435-02-2

DAN GIANCOLA
Powder and Echo. Poems about the American Revolutionary War on Long Island. Introduction by Edward Butscher. $9.95. ISBN 0-963164-0-7

JENNIE HAIR
A Sisterhood of Songs. Poems about women. "Is there some thing/ that makes it necessary for us to be protected—// something implicit/ in the hand under the elbow/ as we cross the street../" In his introduction, Maxwell Corydon Wheat, Jr. says, "Jennie writes with understanding about women and with gentleness about men." $11.00. ISBN 1-886435-00-6

PETER LIPMAN-WULF
Period of Internment: Letters and Drawings from Les Milles 1939-1940. A moving memoir of a German-born American sculptor who was interned at Camp Les Milles in southern France with other German Jews, artists and intellectuals at the outbreak of World War II. $15.00. ISBN 0-963164-5-8

From Canio's Editions

DAVIDA SINGER
Shelter Island Poems. Poems about love and a spiritual journey. "I want to be past you./ as the angle of white sail/ slips across the bay/ just until sunset/ without words and is gone..." Forward by Erika Duncan. $11.00. ISBN 1-886435-01-4

ROB STUART
Similar to Fire. In the Forward to this voume of poetry the poet writes: "Language is the refining fire of my soul, and poetry is its most intimate voice...Poetry is passing the fire hand to hand, soul to soul." Introduction by Perdita Schaffner. $10.95. ISBN 0-963164-2-3

PAT SWEENEY
A Thousand Times and Other Poems. A stunning collection of poems which "celebrate love, sex, a body that is alive, the quickened pulse, the inevitability of longing and desire," as described in the Introduction by R.S. Jones. $10.00. ISBN 0-963164-8-2

SANDRA VREELAND
The Sky Lotto. Poems with an introduction by Barbara Guest who says, "I am shy before these poems written so close to the heart." Vreeland received the Extraordinary Voice Award from Mother's Voices for giving children the opportunity to express their thoughts about AIDS in verse which was then published by The Poetry Society of America. $12.00. ISBN 1-886435-03-0

BEVERLEY WIGGINS WELLS
Simply Black. With a focus upon race and gender, these are poems in which the poet is in touch with a "consciousness empowering me/ to be ultimately whole/ hyphen free/ like the colour of the cosmos/ simply black..." Introduction by Suzanne Gardinier. $10.00. ISBN 0-963164-4-X

* * * * * * * * * * *

For David Ignatow: An Anthology.
Forty-seven poets celebrate the 80th birthday of one of America's most distinguished poets. Among the contributors are Philip Appleman, Marvin Bell, Siv Cedering, Diana Chang, Paul Mariani, Joyce Carol Oates, Diane Wakoski. $10.00. 0-963164-6-6

Ann Chwatsky

About the Author

Fran Castan, a native of Brooklyn, moved to Hong Kong with her six-month-old daughter and her first husband, Sam Castan, when he became Asia bureau chief of *Look* Magazine. He had reported from Vietnam for three years prior to that assignment, but was killed only six months after the couple made their home in the Far East. In the time since, Ms. Castan worked as an editorial assistant at *The New Yorker*, an editor at *Scholastic Magazines* and as editorial director of Learning Corporation, the former educational subsidiary of Columbia Pictures. She first began to write poetry at the age of 40. While earning her M.A. in creative writing at New York University, she won a teaching fellowship, a fellowship to the MacDowell Colony, a prize given by the Academy of American Poets and N.Y.U., and The Lucille Medwick Award from the Poetry Society of America. Her poems have appeared in *Ms.* Magazine and many literary journals and anthologies, including Anchor/ Doubleday's *On Prejudice: A Global Perspective* and Norton's *The Seasons of Women.* For 20 years, Ms. Castan has taught writing and literature at The School of Visual Arts, a college in Manhattan. She lives in Amagansett, New York, with her husband, the painter Lewis Zacks.